Hey Everybody. . .

We teamed up with New Leaf Paper Company to print *Sea Change* on 100% recycled fibers using 100% post consumer waste. We also used soy ink, which produces much less airborne toxins than regular ink. By making these choices we are protecting the environment and saved the following natural resources:

- ✔ 73 full grown trees
- ✔ 34,558 gallons of water
- ✔ 2,313 pounds of solid waste
- ✔ 6,372 pounds of greenhouse gases
- ✔ 33 million BTU's of energy

NEW LEAF PAPER
manufactured with **wind power**

FSC
www.fsc.org
100%
Paper from well-managed forests
FSC® C008955

PRINTED WITH
SOY INK

Publisher certification awarded by Green Press Initiative. www.greenpressinitiative.org

For my wife, Marielle, and two sons, Enzo & Mathéo – J.H.

To my dearest beach buddies Itzel, Ollin & Roan – E.O.

Published by

Freedom Three Publishing
www.freedomthree.com

Project AMPLIFI is a non-profit supporter of *Sea Change*. Project AMPLIFI creates
platforms for music and art to inform, inspire and activate community.
Learn more at www.amplifi.org

ISBN 978-0-9714254-5-3
Library of Congress Control Number: 2015901353

Sea Change was illustrated primarily in watercolor.

Printed in the U.S.A. by Bang Printing.
10 9 8 7 6 5 4 3 2 1
First Edition

Sea Change:

a sudden and dramatic shift,
a positive transformation.

Story by Joel Harper   Illustrated by Erin O'Shea

Let's Work Together!

What will you make?

Share it with us at
www.seachangestory.org

Freedom Three Publishing and Project AMPLIFI are working with a global community of activists toward finding solutions to the challenges facing our oceans. Visit us online to learn more about all the ways you can help our oceans and be inspired by creative artists from around the world that are working with marine litter. If we all pitch in and work together, change is possible. Let's join hands and make a difference for the health of our oceans. Join the Sea Change!

Joel Harper is the author of the award-winning book *All the Way to the Ocean* (Freedom Three Publishing, 2006) He works with various local, national and international environmental organizations and initiatives advocating for marine conservation. When Joel is not writing or publishing books, he can be found enjoying the beautiful shores of Laguna Beach or playing any musical instrument he can get his hands on. Joel lives in Claremont, California with his wife and two sons.

Erin O'Shea is an award-winning illustrator and professor of visual arts. She was raised in a quiet seaside town where she swam, surfed, sailed and worked on the local beaches. The ocean is such a happy place for Erin and her three children that it's a part of their family. They treat the wild and wonderful sea as they would a loved one, with reverence and respect. See more of her work at www.erinoshea.com.